Dear Parent:

Congratulations! Your child is taking the first steps on an exciting journey. The destination? Independent reading!

STEP INTO READING® will help your child get there. The program offers five steps to reading success. Each step includes fun stories and colorful art. There are also Step into Reading Sticker Books, Step into Reading Math Readers, Step into Reading Write-In Readers, Step into Reading Phonics Readers, and Step into Reading Phonics First Steps! Boxed Sets—a complete literacy program with something for every child.

Learning to Read, Step by Step!

Ready to Read   Preschool–Kindergarten
• big type and easy words • rhyme and rhythm • picture clues
For children who know the alphabet and are eager to begin reading.

Reading with Help   Preschool–Grade 1
• basic vocabulary • short sentences • simple stories
For children who recognize familiar words and sound out new words with help.

Reading on Your Own   Grades 1–3
• engaging characters • easy-to-follow plots • popular topics
For children who are ready to read on their own.

Reading Paragraphs   Grades 2–3
• challenging vocabulary • short paragraphs • exciting stories
For newly independent readers who read simple sentences with confidence.

Ready for Chapters   Grades 2–4
• chapters • longer paragraphs • full-color art
For children who want to take the plunge into chapter books but still like colorful pictures.

STEP INTO READING® is designed to give every child a successful reading experience. The grade levels are only guides. Children can progress through the steps at their own speed, developing confidence in their reading, no matter what their grade.

Remember, a lifetime love of reading starts with a single step!

To Larry and Jerre Asel, for always being there
—D.L.H.

For Lorelei
—J.K.

Text copyright © 2008 by David L. Harrison
Illustrations copyright © 2008 by John Kanzler

Published in the United States by Random House Children's Books, a division of Random House, Inc., New York.

Step into Reading, Random House, and the Random House colophon are registered trademarks of Random House, Inc.

Visit us on the Web!
www.stepintoreading.com

Educators and librarians, for a variety of teaching tools, visit us at
www.randomhouse.com/teachers

Library of Congress Cataloging-in-Publication Data
Harrison, David L. (David Lee).
Paul Bunyan : my story / by David L. Harrison ; illustrated by John Kanzler. — 1st ed.
    p. cm. "A step 3 book."
Summary: An introduction to tall tales about the giant lumberjack from the north woods, as told from his own perspective.
ISBN 978-0-375-84688-5 (trade) — ISBN 978-0-375-94688-2 (lib. bdg.)
1. Bunyan, Paul (Legendary character)—Juvenile literature. [1. Bunyan, Paul (Legendary character)—Legends. 2. Folklore—United States. 3. Tall tales.] I. Kanzler, John, ill. II. Title.
PZ8.1.H244Pau 2008 398.2—dc22 [E] 2007051289

Printed in the United States of America   10 9 8 7 6 5 4 3 2 1   First Edition

STEP INTO READING®

STEP 3

Paul Bunyan
My Story

by David L. Harrison

illustrated by John Kanzler

Random House 🏠 New York

Ah, that is much better!

Thank you for opening my book.

A man my size needs room!

But where are my manners?

I am Paul Bunyan.

You can call me Paul.

I come from the North Woods,

where the lumberjacks are

the biggest, best, strongest

lumberjacks in the world.

That is why

I am big and strong, too.

Three hours after I was born,

I already weighed 80 pounds!

When I was one week old,

I wore my daddy's clothes.

My baby buggy
was a lumber wagon
pulled by two oxen.
Wasn't I a cute baby?

You know a growing boy
loves to eat.

Every morning Mama cooked
40 bowls of porridge.

Mmm!

I licked them all clean!

And after that small snack,

I was ready for breakfast.

My voice was growing big, too.

I loved the outdoors so much

that sometimes

I just had to holler,

"Whoooooeeeee!"

And when I hollered,

frogs leaped out of ponds

like they had just sat

on a hot skillet.

I liked winter best of all.

One winter

the North Woods were so cold,

the snow turned blue.

I was out walking

when a baby ox fell into a lake.

SPLASH!

Of course I jumped in
and saved him.

Brrr! That water was cold!

The ox was already blue, too.

He had no mama,

so he followed me home.

I named him Babe.

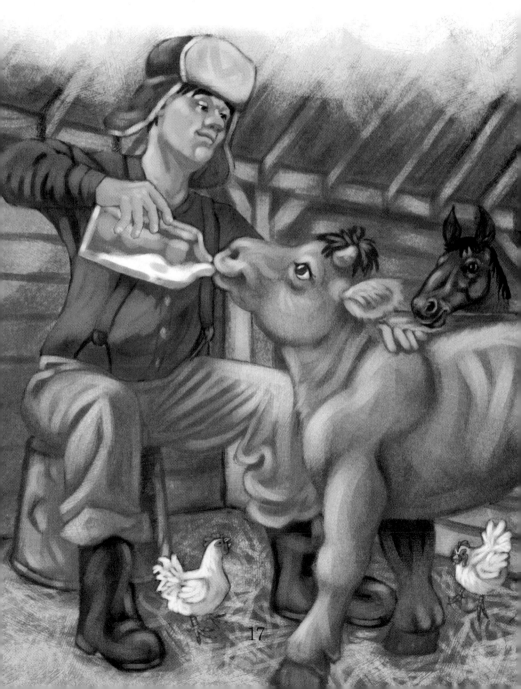

Babe the Blue Ox grew up
the same way I did—BIG!
Between his eyes
Babe is 24 ax handles wide.
When he wants
to nibble something,
he munches 30 bales of hay.
Babe is almost
as strong as I am.

Once we came to a town
that had a crooked road.

Babe pulled that road
so straight,
there were 12 miles left over.

I rolled them up

as a gift for the town.

I grew up to be

the biggest, best, strongest

lumberjack in the world.

I could chop and swing

and haul and clear more trees,

better and faster,

than any man alive.

When other lumberjacks
heard about me,
they wanted to join my crew.
Before long I had
the biggest, best, strongest
crew in the world.

Being a lumberjack is hard,
but it is good work.

Wood from trees

helps build homes and schools

and whole towns.

Folks count on us!

Lumberjacks love to eat!

Sourdough Sam is our cook.

We keep Sam busier

than a mama bear with 50 cubs!

My hungry lumberjacks
eat so many pancakes,
the cookhouse boys
have to wear skates.

You ought to see

Sourdough Sam make soup.

His pot is so big,

he has to row across it.

Once the men are filled up,

it's time for work.

Chop, chop, chop!

My crew just keeps

going and going.

Not even the coldest winter
can stop my crew.
Know why?
They wrap their beards
around themselves
to stay warm
while they work.

35

Thirsty lumberjacks
drink lots of milk.
In the winter we put
green sunglasses
on Lucy the Purple Cow.
She thinks all that snow
is green grass,
so she keeps giving us
sweet milk all winter.

Now let me tell you

about the time

when a bunch of bugs

almost stopped my crew!

Zzzz zzzz zzzz zzzz.

The skeeters were so bad,

my men quit chopping

to swat at them.

I had to do something!

I looked around until I found
some giant bumblebees.
BUZZZ BUZZZ BUZZZ.

I hoped the bumblebees
would fight those skeeters.

But guess what!
The fool things
fell in love instead!

They had children

with stingers at both ends.

BUZZZZ-zzzz-BUZZZZ-zzzz!

We were in real trouble.

Thank goodness
the bumble-skeeters
loved pancake syrup.
It took 300 barrels
of the sticky stuff
to catch them all.

Oh my!

Where has the time gone?

I have to get to work.

I hope you enjoyed

hearing about Babe

and Sam and my crew.

Before I go,

Shhh!

I have a secret just for you.

I am not real!
Real lumberjacks
in the North Woods
made up every one
of these stories
about me.
The stories
helped pass the time
on long, cold winter nights.

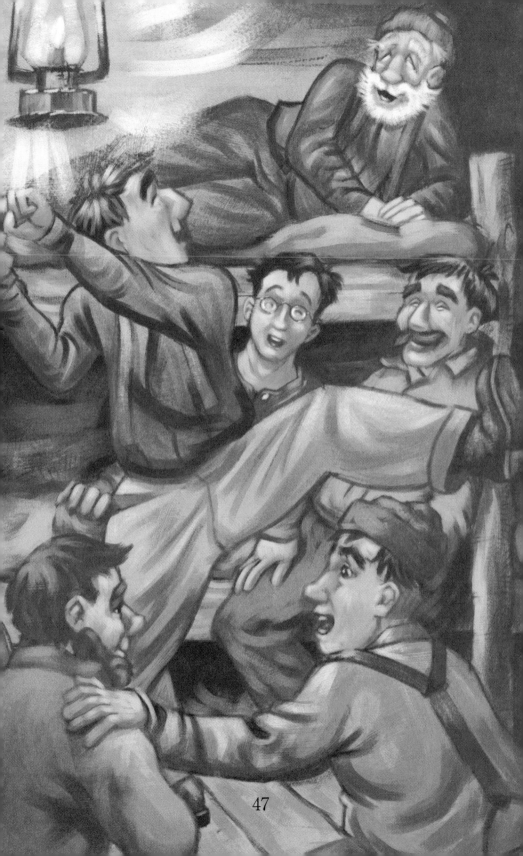

That is fine with me.

As long as folks remember

Paul Bunyan,

the biggest, best, strongest

lumberjack in the world,

I will be right here.

See you in the woods!